To Tony.

I hope y

story

C000116172

# Beyond the Hedge

*Eline Stoye*

Published by

**MELROSE BOOKS**

An Imprint of Melrose Press Limited
St Thomas Place, Ely
Cambridgeshire
CB7 4GG, UK
www.melrosebooks.co.uk

**FIRST EDITION**

Copyright © Eline Stoye 2016

The Author asserts her moral right to
be identified as the author of this work

Front cover image by David Edwards

**ISBN  978-1-911280-84-2**
**epub   978-1-911280-85-9**
**mobi   978-1-911280-86-6**

All rights reserved. No part of this publication may be reproduced, stored in a retrieval system, or transmitted, in any form or by any means electronic, mechanical, photocopying, recording or otherwise, without the prior permission of the publishers.

This book is sold subject to the condition that it shall not, by way of trade or otherwise, be lent, re-sold, hired out or otherwise circulated without the publisher's prior consent in any form of binding or cover other than that in which it is published and without a similar condition including this condition being imposed on the subsequent purchaser.

Printed and bound in Great Britain by:
Lightning Source UK Ltd, Chapter House, Pitfield
Kiln Farm, Milton Keynes, MK11 3LW

# *Dedication*

I would like to dedicate *Beyond the Hedge* to my family: John, my really supportive husband; Trudi and Kerry, my daughters who, like my grandchildren and the children in school, have listened to my stories since they were small; and my grandchildren, Ben, Lily and Brody and, especially, Rebecca who has been wanting me to get my stories published ever since she could read.

Dedication

# Acknowledgements

I would like to thank David Edwards for his charming artwork on the front cover of my book and my publishers, Melrose Books, for their advice and assistance with this, my first children's novel.

# About the Author

Eline Stoye is a semi-retired Primary Teacher, married with two daughters and four grandchildren. After years of making up and telling stories, both to children in school and at home, this is the first story to be produced in book form. "My story is full of mystery and adventure and I hope everyone will enjoy reading it."

# Chapter One

"The taxi's here," Andrew shouted. He had been up since six, had breakfast and now he and Mum were busy getting the suitcases down the stairs.

"I don't see why we have to go to Devon to help someone that nobody knows. Couldn't she get someone else to help her?" Andrew moaned as he dragged his case along the landing.

"I don't want to hear another word, Andrew. Do you hear me?" his mother retorted.

She could understand why he was upset, but she had made up her mind. Eleven-year-old Andrew, his nine-year-old sister, Polly, and their mother, Mary, were Aunt Lizzie's only living relatives and Mary's late husband would have wanted her to look after Aunt Lizzie until she was able to walk again.

Andrew raced back upstairs. He had to go to the toilet before they left.

"Polly, hurry up, or we'll go without you," Andrew moaned as he paced up and down outside the loo. His sister took forever and he had to go before they got on the train.

Mum was outside asking the taxi driver about the price to the station. She had already been round to say her goodbyes to Joy. She was a good neighbour and had promised faithfully to keep an eye on the house.

"Everybody in the taxi, now!" she called, getting the keys out of her bag to lock the front door. Andrew rushed down the stairs and they were soon sitting in the back of the black cab, driving through the busy London streets to Paddington Station.

"Do you think Aunt Lizzie will like us, Andy?" Polly whispered to her brother who was looking out the window at all the tall buildings.

"I don't care if she does or she doesn't," he replied. He was still fuming at having to miss playing in the school football match that coming Saturday.

"Do you think we'll have to go to school in Devon if she doesn't get better quickly?" Polly asked again.

"Mum won't make us stay that long," he replied, but inside he wasn't sure. The thought of moving to Devon permanently hadn't crossed his mind. *If that happens*, he thought to himself, *I'm off!*

Soon the taxi was pulling off the road into the station. The station was really large and there were so many people rushing in and out. Everybody seemed to be in a hurry.

"Right, love. That'll be £10," the taxi driver said as he put the last suitcase on the pavement.

"Andrew, go and get a trolley. We can't carry these ourselves," Mum instructed and, before long, they were standing in a long queue waiting for the train to the West Country to arrive. People stood patiently outside the platform. Most of them had trolleys laden with suitcases, or heavy bags.

There was a train standing on the next platform and the children watched as those passengers walked along, searching for their carriages. So many stressed faces! Suddenly, a whistle blew and they saw a guard wave a flag. In no time, the huge diesel engine began to pull the carriages out of the station. They could see some people on the train were still trying to find their seats as the train slowly disappeared out of sight.

"Hey," Andrew shouted, pulling his mother's sleeve, "is that our train?"

He had been watching the other train disappearing into the distance when he'd realised there was a train rolling towards them, on his side of the platform. As it approached, the people in the queue started fumbling for their tickets and checking to see if they had all their luggage. Polly had an urgent need to go to the toilet again, but Mum said it was too late. Polly started dancing up and down, much to everyone's annoyance.

"Keep still, Polly. You can go when we're on the train," Mum said as she looked in her bag for the tickets.

The people in the queue surged forward towards the barrier and soon they were all hurrying along the platform.

"It's J, Andrew," Mum called as he ran along the train. There were more than twenty carriages, but it wasn't long before they found theirs.

"Can I help you with those?" asked a middle-aged man as he watched Mum struggling to put the suitcases on the rack.

"Thank you," Mum replied.

"If you need to get them down again, please don't hesitate to ask," he said, smiling at the children.

Andrew and Polly sat down quickly. The journey was about to begin.

There was no turning back now.

# Chapter Two

No sooner had they settled in their seats than the carriage lurched forward and the train began moving out of the station. Andrew watched as it gathered speed, passing factories and houses until they finally left the big city behind. He felt a little sad at leaving his friends but, hopefully, they would be back in London again soon. He hadn't ever been to the country before and had never seen so many fields and trees, but soon he was bored with the view. He had packed some comics, but they were up in his suitcase.

He looked at the other passenger. The man was reading his paper. He looked interesting. He watched as the man turned another page. He smiled at the boy, but Andrew looked away. He didn't talk to strangers, especially now. He looked at the man through the reflection in the carriage window. He was wearing half glasses and he had a black moustache. Not many men he knew had a moustache. Andrew's imagination began working overtime. The man looked suspicious. His brown trousers and corduroy jacket were not usual either. Obviously, he was up to no good. Andrew had read about spies who looked like ordinary people. He wondered what was in the black bag that the man kept close to his legs.

"Is it time to eat, Mum?" Polly whispered. She was always hungry!

"Excuse me," Mum looked at the stranger. "I wonder if I could trouble you to get my case down again?" She felt a little awkward at asking, but the food was in the case. The man folded his paper again and took the case off the rack.

"Are the animals ready for feeding then?" he asked, grinning at Andrew who scowled back. A few minutes later, when the packed lunch had been given out, they all settled down to eat.

"Would you like one?" Polly asked, leaning forward, pushing her cheese sandwiches under the man's nose. Andrew stared at his sister. He wasn't prepared to share his food with anyone!

"Thank you very much," he replied. "It's very kind of you, but I've already eaten."

*Thank goodness for that*, Andrew thought. Knowing Mum, she would have insisted that he shared his lunch as well!

It wasn't long before their little meal was over and, having put the case under her seat, Mum settled back for a nap.

Andrew and Polly had been playing Hangman, but Polly stopped playing as she was bored.

"Let's play 'I Spy'," she shouted.

"No!" Andrew snapped. Then they started arguing.

Suddenly, putting down his newspaper, the man with black moustache leaned forward. "Shh ... you will wake your mother. Let me see what I've got in my bag."

He took some playing cards out and began shuffling them. Andrew was disappointed. He could have at least had a pistol in the case, but all he could see was a pile of papers. He couldn't be a spy after all.

Polly moved over to sit next to the stranger as he showed them some card tricks. He said his name was Simon and he was, in fact, a teacher.

Just their luck, Andrew thought, out of all the carriages on the train to choose from, a teacher had to choose theirs. Still he was really good at card tricks!

The hours passed quickly now. They passed towns and villages and, while the children slept, both adults chatted enthusiastically about their expectations in a new county. However, it wasn't long before Simon was packing his things away.

The train pulled into Exeter station and they waved as he walked away down the platform.

"Not far now," Mum said as the train pulled out of the station again.

"We've been on this train all day," Andrew said stretching his legs. "I'm hungry."

But Mum wasn't listening. She was thinking about Aunt Lizzie and how she was going to help her. *The old lady must be so frustrated at breaking her leg*, she thought.

Before long, the train was pulling into their station. Simon had already taken their cases down before he had left the train, so they were able to lift them off onto the platform themselves.

"Right, let's find a taxi," Mum said as they carried the luggage out into the street.

"There's one," Andrew said, pointing to a black car that was parked on the corner.

They hurried over and, while the driver put the cases in the boot, Mum read out the address.

"Did you say Ireton House?" the man said giving her a curious look. Mum nodded.

"We don't get many people go there," Andrew and Polly looked at each other. What did he mean?

# Chapter Three

The road to Ireton House was narrow and windy and by the time they arrived it was almost dark. The taxi turned off the road and passed through a pair of enormous ornate gates and went up a long, gravel drive. The driver pulled up outside a large building, the outline of its chimneys standing eerily against the darkening sky.

"Here we are then," the taxi driver said as he got out of the car. "Can't remember the last time I had to come here. It must have been when the old master was alive. Strange place, if you ask me," he mumbled as he put the cases on the step.

Mum wasn't really listening. She was too busy trying to get change out of her purse.

"I'll wait until you are settled," the taxi driver said as Mum went up the steps to knock on the large wooden door.

Andrew and Polly stood very still. They were both tired and a little scared. Suddenly, the door opened to reveal a middle-aged woman holding a large candlestick, the flames flickering wildly in the draught of the door.

"Come in, my lovelies," she said, smiling at the children. "I'm sorry we've got no electricity, been out since this afternoon." The woman ushered them in through the door and into the hall. It was a large space with several doors leading off from it and right in the middle was an enormous staircase. The top of the stairs was in darkness, so it was impossible to see the landing. Both children felt uneasy as they listened to the woman.

"My name is Mrs James," she continued, "and I come up from the village twice a week to do a bit of cleaning. Your aunt sends her apologies, she has gone to bed and will see you in the morning. Terrible thing, her falling down the stairs like she did. Good thing she has you here now. She lives all alone in this old house, much too big for her, I say," and, as she spoke, she beckoned them to follow her through an open door into the kitchen.

It wasn't long before they were all tucking into a hot meal and then Mrs James led them up the grand staircase onto the landing to find their bedrooms.

"This place gives me the creeps," Polly whispered as they walked along the landing.

Andrew nodded. He was trying not to look at the paintings that hung either side of the walls. It was dark and the candlelight made things look really scary, but he could just make out that they were of people and he felt that they were watching them as they passed by. A shudder went down his back. He had a bad feeling about Ireton House!

"It won't take you long to find your way around. Your aunt doesn't use the West wing anymore, not since her husband died. No call to go there now. Mind you, I wouldn't go nosing around there. She gets a bit funny about anyone doing that," she went on, looking straight at the children. "Here we are. Now I'll leave you to get comfortable. Goodnight," and with that, she turned around and walked back to the stairs.

Suddenly, the electricity came on again revealing a large room with two single beds, a wardrobe and two chests of drawers. The bathroom was next door.

"You'll be fine now," Mum reassured them after she had made sure they were ready for bed.

"I'll leave the light on. My room is just across the landing," Mum said reassuringly. She kissed them both goodnight then turned the bedroom light off and went downstairs.

"I wonder what that taxi driver meant," Andrew whispered, but Polly couldn't hear him. She was so tired and the bed was so comfy that she had fallen asleep almost immediately and, before long, Andrew joined her.

In the meantime, Mum was downstairs talking to Mrs James. It seemed that Aunt Lizzie had broken her leg in two places and wouldn't be able to move around independently for some time.

"The old lady hasn't been well since her husband passed away. She doesn't talk about it, but we think she has money problems and this old house costs so much to run. I'm glad she was able to get in touch with you." It was obvious that Mrs James felt uncomfortable speaking about her employer's affairs, but she had worked for Aunt Lizzie for years and cared about her.

"Don't worry, dear," Mum tried to reassure her. "We'll stay as long our aunt needs us."

# Chapter Four

Andrew was the first awake. He jumped out of bed, rushed to the window and threw open the thick curtains.

"Wow!" he shouted.

"What's the matter?" Polly sighed. "You woke me up."

"You should see the garden. It's massive," Andrew said as he began putting on his clothes. "I'm going out to explore."

Polly watched as he ran to the bedroom door and then she heard him chasing down the stairs. She wasn't ready to go outside. All she was interested in was finding her mother and having breakfast. She was hungry again – exploring could wait!

"Yes, you can go outside," Mum was telling Andrew as Polly walked in the kitchen later. "But remember, this is not our house. Don't break anything, ok?"

"Yes, Mum", Andrew answered and, grabbing his football from the shelf, he was gone.

"And what about you, Polly?" Mum said as she poured some cereal in a bowl.

"I'll stay and help you," Polly said, taking the bowl. Polly wanted to get to know her aunt and she had lots of questions to ask her, especially about the horses!

Meanwhile, out in the garden, Andrew was searching every-where for a gate. There wasn't one. The garden and the fields beyond all belonged to the house. It was perfect for playing football. He ran about and then started dribbling his ball along the edge of a large hedge which ran down one side of the house. He knew he could improve his dribbling skills in no time in this garden. Maybe it had been a good idea to come after all.

Suddenly, his ball bounced through a hole in the hedge.

Without thinking, Andrew climbed through to get it. He had expected to find his ball straight away but, instead of there being a field on the other side of the hedge, Andrew found himself in the middle of a narrow country lane.

"That's really weird," he said out loud.

"What is?" came a voice from behind him. Andrew spun around with a start. There, in front of him, was a strange boy. He was dressed in a dirty shirt and trousers and he had a piece of old rope tied round his waist. Andrew thought he was a little older than him, probably about fourteen or fifteen.

"Well, what's weird?" the boy continued.

"Nothing," Andrew replied, "have you seen a football about here?" he asked.

The young lad laughed. "What sort of ball did you say?"

"A football," Andrew retorted, "you know, a ball to kick." Andrew was losing his patience.

The strange boy looked at him but then, without saying another word, he turned around and walked away.

Andrew stared after him. He seemed to drift into the distance and then disappear.

*How rude*, he thought, but he soon forgot about the stranger. He was too busy searching for his ball. Then he saw it. It was by the hole in the hedge. How did he miss it? He grabbed the ball and scrambled back into the garden.

"Where does the lane on the other side of the big hedge go to?" Andrew asked Auntie Lizzie later when they were having tea.

"What lane, dear?" she replied. "There are only fields on the other side of the hedge. No lanes."

"But there is a lane. I spoke to a lad who was walking down it." Andrew was quite determined that he was right.

Auntie Lizzie looked puzzled. "What did this young lad look like?" she asked quietly.

Andrew described the lad and commented on his shabby,

11

old-fashioned clothes.

"You must have been mistaken, dear," she insisted.

Mum gave Andrew her special look that told him not to mention it again.

"There is a lane," Andrew told Polly later as they climbed the stairs on the way to bed. "I'll take you there tomorrow."

# Chapter Five

Andrew was up early. He was determined to find the gap in the hedge again.

He ran over to Polly's bed and gave her a good shake.

"Wake up, Polly," he shouted. "Let's go down before everyone is awake."

Polly was too tired.

"You go," she yawned. "I'm not awake yet," and turned over.

"Ok," he said and grabbed his clothes.

It was really misty when he got outside and he could barely see the hedge.

There was a strange smell in the air as well. He hadn't noticed it the day before. Maybe it was coming from the farm down the road.

As he started to walk along the edge of the hedge, the mist grew thicker. Soon he couldn't see the house anymore.

"I know the gap's here somewhere," he said to himself as he pulled at the hedging.

He was determined to prove his aunt wrong – he hadn't imagined the lane and he hadn't imagined the boy.

"Yes!" There it was. Andrew pushed his way through the gap and again found himself in the lane, but this time it was deserted.

He looked up and down. He hadn't thought about where the lane led to, but he wanted to find the boy.

Suddenly, he heard the sound of horses' hooves and the rumbling of wheels. He looked round just in time to see a coach and four horses hurtling down the lane towards him. There was no time to get out of the way so, instinctively, he fell to the ground and covered his head with his hands.

13

Then the strangest thing happened. He heard something pass over him and then, looking up, he saw the coach rumbling down the lane into the distance. It had gone right over him but, amazingly, he hadn't been touched. He got to his feet and watched it disappear. How could that have happened?

"What was that?" he said in disbelief.

"That was my uncle," a voice said and there, standing beside him, was the boy. "I'm glad you came back," he went on, "I hoped you would."

Andrew stared at him and then looked down the lane at the coach. Was he dreaming?

"I think I should be going," he said looking anxiously back towards the hedge.

"But, don't you want to know more about why I wanted you to come back?" the boy asked.

Andrew felt a little afraid. Maybe the boy and all the other happenings were not real, but was it really possible that he was talking to a ghost?

"Please stay a while. Let me show you ..." and with that, he began walking down the lane, beckoning for Andrew to follow. He led him to a derelict cottage. Nobody could have lived there for decades.

The windows were broken and the front door was hanging off its hinges. Andrew could smell the strange smell even more now – smoke, there were burned pieces of wood everywhere. There had once been a fire, that's why the cottage was in such a bad way.

"This is my home," the boy said as he passed through the doorway into the charred remains of a living room.

Andrew stared at him.

"*Nobody could live here*," Andrew thought to himself, looking around the room.

"I want you to help me," the boy went on. "You have come to stay at the big house and I need you to find something there, something important."

"Why can't you go there yourself?" Andrew asked.

"I would, but I am locked in the spirit of the garden and cannot enter the house until my name is cleared," the boy spoke in earnest. "Please help me so that I may regain my good name and move on."

'Spirit of the garden', what did he mean?

"You are a ghost, aren't you?" Andrew muttered, not sure if he would like the answer.

"I am the spirit of your ancestor, Andrew, and I ask for your help. I have waited a long time for you to come. I know you are here for a purpose," the ghost sighed.

Andrew was right. The boy was a ghost.

But then, suddenly, he heard a familiar sound. It was his mother calling him.

"I'll be back," he called as he ran out of the cottage and back along to the gap in the hedge.

His mother was waiting by a large oak tree on the other side of the hedge.

"I don't mind you being out in the garden, but don't forget we are guests in this house and Auntie Lizzie gets concerned if you disappear for hours!"

As they walked up to the house, Andrew tried to tell his mother about the strange boy.

"There is a lane beyond the hedge. Please come and see for yourself," he begged her.

"Alright," his mother said, "I'll come with you tomorrow, after lunch. You can show it to me when I have finished my chores. Auntie will be having her afternoon nap." She knew Andrew would keep on pestering her until she agreed to come with him. "Why don't you help Polly in the library tomorrow? She's sorting out some old books. If you do that, we can all go after lunch."

Andrew knew there had to be a catch, but he agreed.

# Chapter Six

After breakfast, the children made their way to the library. As they walked down the corridor, Andrew was thinking about the ghost boy. How could he help him?

Perhaps he would speak to Mum when they went back to the garden. Andrew wasn't looking forward to tidying up old books, but he had promised. Still, he didn't have to rush, did he? He was studying the decor of the hall as he walked along, especially the grand staircase. There were different coloured birds on the wallpaper of the hall and, next to the stairs, stood a grandfather clock. He remembered Mum saying something about how Auntie Lizzie had admired the clock, although it hadn't worked for years. She had told Mum that the clock had belonged to the Aldertons who were distant relatives of Aunt Lizzie's husband. They had been rich landowners in the area in the 18th century and many rumours had arisen about the youngest son and the lost family jewels. She had said that the house was built on the foundations of the original mansion that had belonged to the Aldertons – only the West Wing had survived.

Andrew stared at the clock. What if it was true? What if the ghost boy had wanted him to find the missing jewels?

"Are you going to help me, Andrew, or just stand there!" Polly shouted from the library.

"Coming!" he shouted back. Treasure hunting would have to wait.

The books in the library were very dusty. Most of them were very old and the children had to be very careful.

"I haven't found one book that I'd want to read," Polly said wearily. "They didn't have books for children in the olden days."

Andrew wasn't really listening. He was thinking about the afternoon when they were all going back to the garden.

Suddenly, as he reached up towards the shelf to put a book back, he lost his balance and the book fell to the floor.

"What are you doing?" Polly yelled at him. "That book must be really valuable!"

"I slipped," he replied, but as he picked up the large volume of Chaucer, a crumpled piece of paper fell out. It looked very old.

Andrew grabbed it quickly and stuffed it in his pocket.

"Where are you going now?" Polly moaned as he headed for the library door.

"I've got to get something," he replied and, with that, he ran back upstairs to their bedroom.

Shutting the bedroom door, he took the paper out of his pocket and tried to read what was written on it.

The paper was a kind of parchment and it was headed with some sort of crest.

It appeared to be a letter written in 'Old English' but the ink had faded with age so it was impossible for Andrew to understand.

He would have to show the paper to the boy. Perhaps he would know what it said.

Disappointedly, he folded it carefully and put it back in his pocket. Suddenly, the bedroom door opened and Polly steamed in.

"You promised to help me this morning. What are you doing?" she looked at him suspiciously.

"Nothing," he replied, "I was just coming."

"Lunch time," Mum called from the kitchen.

"OK!" They both shouted.

# Chapter Seven

The walk along the hedge with Mum and Polly seemed to go on forever.

"It's not far now," Andrew said, trying to remember where the gap was.

"Andrew, I have to get back in a minute," Mum said, checking her watch.

"It's here," Andrew shouted, clambering through the hedge. "Come on."

Both Polly and his mother climbed after him, but there was no lane for them to see. They stared at the field of barley in front of them. Andrew was staring too. He couldn't believe it.

"Andrew, that's the last time you bring me out on one of your imaginary capers," Mum said as she scrambled back through the hedge.

"But I didn't," Andrew implored. "There is a lane." But it was too late, both Polly and his mother were on their way back to the house.

"They never believe us, do they?" Andrew spun around to see the boy standing behind him. He was munching something.

"Want one?" he asked, offering Andrew a rather overripe apple.

Andrew declined his offer. He was confused. Why was it that when the others were there nothing happened and now that he was alone, the lane was clear for everyone to see.

"Coming?" the boy asked as he looked back to Andrew.

The cottage was just as cold and dirty as the day before and Andrew couldn't help but feel sorry for the boy.

"What's your name?" he asked as the ghost invited him inside.

"My name was Joshua Alderton. My father was the Earl of Penmire and he owned the mansion and all the land for miles around."

Joshua went on to tell him how he had had a very happy childhood until he was twelve when his mother and older brothers and sisters died of the plague.

"This had a terrible effect on my father," he continued. "He shut himself away from everyone and I hardly saw him for months until one morning, when I was summoned to his rooms to meet his brother … my Uncle Reuben.

"My father had never mentioned having a brother before and it now seemed this man was to take over the running of the estate and, worst of all, he was to take the responsibility of me." Joshua gave a great sigh as he said this and Andrew saw a look of fear come over his face.

"From the moment my uncle came to live at the house, my life changed," he said. "The servants, who had been my companions for years, were denied me and I spent many lonely hours wandering here in the garden as I was refused access to the house except for food. I wasn't even allowed the pleasure of riding, my great passion at that time. My father had no control over what was happening to me. He didn't even know that I had been banished to live in the gatehouse which is where we are now. Eventually, sometime later, I was summoned back to the house to be told that my father had died. In disbelief, I was led to the great hall where his body lay. I can't tell you how much I cried for my dead father, but then my uncle was very quick to inform me that he was now the rightful heir to the house and the estate and he was making arrangements for me to pursue a life at sea. I couldn't believe it. My father would never have disinherited me! However, the papers he thrust at me looked genuine. I was not to know that he had filled my father's mind with stories of how bad I was … 'a good for nothing boy who couldn't be trusted'."

"What happened to you?" Andrew asked. "Did you go to sea?"

"No, Andrew, the night I was to be whisked away, I sneaked back into the house to find my mother's jewels – I could not let my uncle have them. I knew they would still be in her bureau as my father had left her things exactly as they were when she died. I managed to get past the servants' quarters, up to her room and let myself in, closing the door quietly behind me. Tearfully, I found the jewellery box and, putting it in a sack, I slipped back out of the house again. I ran as fast as I could back to the gatehouse, but when I opened the box it was empty, save for this," and with that he placed a tiny velvet pouch in Andrew's hand.

Andrew opened it to reveal a large, dirty stone. He was holding an uncut diamond, but as he had never seen a precious jewel before, he, disappointedly, put it back in the pouch.

"What had happened to the jewels?" he asked, giving the pouch back to the ghost.

"I can only assume the jewels are still in the house," the ghost said, "and that is why I want you to help me find them. Some men," he went on, "came later in the evening and, instead of taking me off to sea, they knocked me unconscious and torched the gatehouse. I died in the flames and my uncle spread the rumour that I had run off to sea, taking the jewels with me."

Andrew felt angry at this. Now he was even more determined to help Joshua and vowed he would do everything he could to find the jewels and clear his name.

Suddenly, he remembered the piece of paper.

"I found an old piece of paper in a book this morning," he said anxiously, "but I have left it back at the house. I couldn't read the writing and it had a strange drawing on it."

"Does it look like this?" the ghost asked, showing him a similar drawing on the back of a chair.

"Yes," Andrew replied.

"That is our family crest. I would be interested to see it. Maybe, it was written by my father," the ghost said, looking wistfully towards the garden.

It was supper time by the time Andrew got back to the house again.

"Right then, Andrew," Mum said as he came in the back door, "you will not be going out in the garden tomorrow. You are confined to the house. There are lots of jobs waiting for you!" She was still very cross with him for wasting her time.

Andrew tried to look unhappy at this news, but secretly he was pleased. Now he had the chance to explore the house and to, hopefully, find the lost jewels.

# *Chapter Eight*

The next morning, Andrew got up early. He had his breakfast and listened carefully while Mum gave him his instructions.

"There are enough things on this," she said, handing him a list, "to keep you busy all day, and, if they're not finished, then you will carry on with them tomorrow. By the way, Polly and I will be taking Auntie Lizzie to the hospital this afternoon and we'll be out for a while as I need to do some shopping. I expect to see lots of 'gleaming silver' and a really tidy house when I come back. Do you understand?" she asked pointedly.

Andrew nodded and then, list in hand, he went off back to the library.

As he walked past the dining room he overheard Auntie Lizzie talking to Mrs James: "I'm afraid, Sarah, that I won't be able to keep you on much longer," she said anxiously. "I have been advised that it would be better for me to find some smaller accommodation in the village and the house will have to be sold."

Mrs James looked at her sadly.

"It won't be the same, not coming here to help you out," she said, touching Auntie Lizzie's arm, "but perhaps it will be for the best." She didn't know what to say to Auntie Lizzie; she could see how upset she was and knew she didn't want to leave Ireton House.

"Don't you worry yourself, dear. I'll be able to come and see you more often if you live in the village and you'll be able to see more of the ladies from the WI, so it might not be so bad," she said, reaching for the kettle. "Now, just sit yourself down and I'll make you a nice cup of tea."

Auntie Lizzie watched as Mrs James got on with the tea. She

hadn't told her everything. As much as Mrs James had grown to be a friend rather than an employee, she couldn't tell her that the bank was going to repossess the house in two months' time. When her husband died, there was no insurance policy to finish paying the outstanding mortgage and she had been desperately trying to make the payments out of her pension, but it was impossible. The bank manager had been very sympathetic, but he made her realise that she couldn't go on getting deeper and deeper in debt, so there was no other solution but to let the house go.

Andrew had made his way to the library before Mrs James could see him. He had been surprised to hear what Auntie Lizzie had said. He wondered if Mum knew and whether he should tell her. However, his thoughts were soon interrupted.

"I knew you'd be in trouble," Polly smirked, handing him a duster as he walked in. "Mum was fuming yesterday. I'm glad you have to carry on helping me, I'm getting bored with cleaning and tidying on my own!"

The children spent the entire morning working in the library, but Andrew didn't mind. He couldn't wait till the afternoon when everyone would be out of the house. He had decided to explore the West Wing. He had asked Auntie Lizzie about this part of the house earlier in the week and she had said that part of the West Wing was, in fact, three hundred years old, but she had said it was off limits because some parts weren't very safe. Her husband had fallen there and his injuries had led to his eventual death. Andrew didn't feel phased by this; after all he was much younger and fitter!

Promptly after lunch, everyone got in a taxi and Andrew watched as it drove off down the drive and out of sight. His heart was pounding wildly. In a flash, he raced up the stairs and along the landing until he came to the door to the West Wing. For a moment or two he stared at the door and then, clutching the handle firmly, he pulled it open.

In front of him was an empty room; no furniture, no fittings, only a large open fireplace. Andrew stepped in gingerly, remembering about his great uncle, and walked over to the window. He could see the hedge from this side of the building and the garden looked a little different from above. There were more flower beds than he remembered and he could see a stable block over in the distance. He didn't remember that being there before, but he hadn't been everywhere in the garden, so it didn't worry him.

He turned to look at the fireplace. It was obviously made of stone, but it was full of ornate carvings. Andrew recognised the Alderton crest imprinted in the mantle while statues of dragons and other strange creatures occupied the hearth. They looked so strange that he couldn't resist touching them.

Suddenly, as he ran his hand over the head of one of the dragons, the floor of the hearth opened up, revealing a stone staircase. Andrew stared at it in horror. What had he done?

Then, remembering why he was there, he stepped cautiously down the steps.

He found himself in another room, very like the one above, but this room was full of fine furniture and amazing things. There were all kinds of Chinese-style ornaments: silk screens, candelabras, ornate bureaus, fine tapestries on the walls and everything he could have imagined that would be in the house of a rich gentleman living in the 18th century. There was a long table, laden with fine china and gold cutlery. Andrew could only stand and stare in wonder at it all. Then, quickly regaining his thoughts, he began searching for any sign of the missing jewels. He was so busy with his search that he hadn't noticed the room was getting darker and colder. Suddenly, his concentration was interrupted.

"What right have you to be here?" a voice boomed from the far end of the room.

Andrew spun round to see the spectre of a tall man, dressed in a brocade jacket, silk shirt and leggings. He was wearing a powdered wig and he carried a large whip which he pointed menacingly towards him.

Andrew gulped. He knew immediately who the figure was. It was Joshua's Uncle Reuben.

"I was lost, sir," he mumbled, edging his way back towards the steps.

"Lost! Well, we'll see about that. You're just another meddling brat like my nephew. I soon disposed of him and I can easily do the same for you," the ghost snarled as he began gliding towards Andrew.

"Never!" Andrew screamed and raced for the steps. He had never run so fast in his life before, but he made it back into the empty room and headed for the door. Then, wrenching it open, he dived back onto the landing and slammed the door behind him.

From inside the room, he could hear the ghost ranting and raving and then, all was silent.

His mind was racing. Had the ghost intended to hurt him?

Waiting a minute or two, he carefully opened the door and looked in. The room was as it was before – empty, except for the large fireplace. The steps had disappeared and there was no sound to be heard. Andrew carefully closed the door again and walked slowly back down the stairs to the kitchen. He was still shaking, but he knew he had to get on with the jobs; his mother would be back soon and it had to look as if he had done some work.

If only he could tell her what had happened, but he knew there was no point – she wouldn't believe him!

He sat down at the table and began cleaning the silver.

He would have to tell Joshua what had happened, but when?

# Chapter Nine

Although it was the beginning of August, leaves were beginning to change colour and a chilly autumnal wind was blowing amongst the trees as Andrew made his way back to the hedge after lunch the next day. He had successfully finished the jobs that Mum had given him, so he was allowed back outside for a while. He had remembered the old paper and he couldn't wait to tell the ghost what had happened in the West wing.

However, surprisingly, there was no sign of Joshua on the other side of the hedge, so he decided to walk along to the cottage. As he walked down the lane, he was wondering what the ghost would say about his meeting with his uncle and whether he'd say to go back. To his disappointment, the cottage was deserted when he finally got there.

"Joshua, where are you?" he called, but there was no reply.

He was confused. He didn't know whether to wait or to go back; it was the first time Joshua had not appeared and he felt a little afraid. Had something happened to him?

"Nothing can happen to a ghost," he said reassuringly to himself and turned to leave.

Suddenly, there was a glow of light and the ghost boy appeared in the doorway.

"I am sorry I was not here when you arrived, I was exercising Sultan. Come," he said, leading Andrew outside and there, much to Andrew's amazement, tethered to a fence, stood the spectre of a pure white horse. "I told you I loved riding," he continued. "Sultan has been my constant companion for most of my time in the garden," he stroked the horse's head affectionately as he spoke and the horse, in turn, shook his head and looked round at Andrew, who had started telling Joshua about meeting his uncle.

"I was so scared," Andrew went on. He wanted to stroke Sultan, too, but he knew that would be impossible.

The ghost smiled. "Remember, Andrew, he cannot hurt you. He is just a spectre."

"Also," Andrew continued, "my aunt has money problems. I heard her telling the housekeeper that the house will have to be sold."

Joshua looked at him. He could not bear the thought of his home belonging to anyone but family.

"I want you to go back to the West Wing, Andrew," he said, "I remember my father showing me a small oriental pot that he had been given by the Prince Regent on the occasion of a special ball that had been held at our home. My father had been favoured by the Prince Regent and, as he was a great collector of all things oriental, the prince had given this small trinket to my father for his loyalty. It was a fine pot, covered in delicate drawings of birds and flowers and I remember my father saying it was very precious. Maybe, if you can find it, it will help your aunt to stay.

I know you will feel afraid, but remember, my uncle cannot hurt you. He is just a spectre. Now," he said mounting Sultan, "we must finish our ride."

Andrew thanked him and was just about to leave when he remembered the paper.

"Stop! Just before you go," he said anxiously, "I forgot to give you this," and he handed it to Joshua who dismounted again to scan it carefully.

"Yes, it is from my father," he said tearfully as he read the contents.

"My dearest son, they say I have only days to live so we may not meet again in this life. I have always been so proud of you and want you to know this. Your Uncle Reuben has said such terrible things about you, but I believe none of it. I have instructed John to place your mother's jewels in a very safe place for you to find when I am gone. I know you are good at riddles so the clues will be no problem for you. My eyes have weakened and I am not sure what the papers were that I signed for your uncle but, whatever happens, I know the jewels will be safe for you to find.

God bless you, my son, and give you a long and happy life.

Your loving father.

"I am so grateful that you have found this," he said, holding the paper close to his chest, "I always knew my father cared about me and I never doubted he would have ignored my uncle. My love of riddles may help to find the jewels, but the clues are hard. I may need your help."

"I'm not very good at riddles," Andrew sighed, "but, if you give me a clue, I'll try to solve it."

"Very well," the ghost said, "this is the last clue … 'Look where time stands still'. The other clues I will try to solve myself."

Andrew repeated the clue over and over on his way back to the hedge. He had no idea what it meant, but he knew it was important.

The thought of going back to the West Wing was really worrying him. He trusted Joshua, but he felt that Uncle Reuben would do everything to prevent him solving the clue and finding the tiny pot that Joshua had described.

Did he have enough courage to continue the search?

# *Chapter Ten*

There was lots of excitement in the house after supper. Auntie Lizzie had invited some ladies from the village WI to come over for a meeting and, as it was the first time she had walked without her plaster, she was very anxious that she could show them that she was recovering.

"I've missed going down to the village to see my friends," she was telling Mum as they prepared a small buffet, "and I like seeing the different people that we invite to speak at the meetings."

That night, she had arranged for a medium to come to the house. "They say she's very good and she lives locally, so we didn't have to pay her very much. You will join us, Mary, won't you?"

Mum wasn't too sure. She didn't believe in such things and was very nervous of the whole idea. Still, her aunt would need help with the catering so she agreed.

Andrew and Polly were introduced to the ladies when they arrived and then, without seeing the 'special guest speaker', they were ushered into the study where they could watch television. This was a treat as Auntie Lizzie didn't believe in children staying up late.

Andrew had other plans, however. He knew Mum would be busy helping Auntie Lizzie and no one would be interested in him and Polly with the medium around, so he could go back to the secret room without any worry. He felt a little stronger about meeting Uncle Reuben again, but as Joshua had said, he couldn't hurt him. He decided that this was an ideal time to continue his search.

"Where are you going?" Polly asked as he got up to go.

"To the toilet!" he replied sharply. Polly could be so annoying at times. He would have told her all about the room and the ghosts, but as she hadn't believed him when he said about the lane, there was no point!

Once up in the bedroom, Andrew got his torch and the notepad on which he'd written the clue. He stared at the words again – 'Look where time stands still'. Well, the West Wing was three hundred years old and the secret room looked as though it hadn't changed since then, so it had to hold the answer. Maybe if he found the oriental pot, he would be nearer to solving the clue as well.

The landing light was off when he left the bedroom. He could hear the ladies downstairs laughing and chatting as he walked along. The people in the family portraits still seemed to stare at him as he passed, but this time he didn't feel as scared as before. He kept remembering Joshua's words – 'he cannot hurt you' – as he opened the door to the empty room and went inside again. However, once inside the room his fear returned.

The electricity was turned off, so it was really lucky that he'd remembered his torch. As he walked over to the fireplace, the torchlight created strange shadows on the walls and the shape of the dragons loomed eerily above him as he tried to remember which dragon's head he had touched before. His heart was beating furiously as he stroked each one, their stone eyes lighting up menacingly in the torchlight.

"You can do this," he whispered to himself as the steps appeared and he stepped slowly down into the secret room. He was filled with dread as he shone the torch around the walls and around the items of furniture. He knew Uncle Reuben was in the room. He could feel the cold air.

*I am not afraid of a silly old ghost*, he kept repeating in his head, as he began looking in the nearest cupboard. The torchlight filled the immediate area, but everything was pitch black beyond it. He scanned the top shelf: it was full of fine gold cups and plates. The Alderton crest was on everything and, as he moved each one aside, Andrew began to lose his fears. He knew he would have to check everything in the room, so there was no time to be afraid!

As he searched in each unit of furniture, he completely lost all sense of time and he had forgotten about getting back to the study before Mum found out he was missing.

The largest bureau was finely carved with strange animals and birds. It was the only bureau he hadn't looked in. As he pulled open one of the small drawers he saw a ring, a beautiful gold, diamond-encrusted ring lying on some linen napkins.

"It's one of the jewels!" he said aloud. "The rest of the jewels must be here."

He picked up the ring and tried it on. It fitted. It was as though it was made for him.

Suddenly, an icy breeze blew across his face and he felt something tugging at his finger.

"You will never have it!" Uncle Reuben screamed into his ear and he then knew that he wasn't as protected as Joshua had said. Two evil eyes stared through the darkness at him and, suddenly, it was as though two unseeing hands had grabbed him by the shoulders and he was being propelled towards the window. The ghost meant to destroy him!

"Andrew, where are you? I know you're here. Come out this instant!" It was Mum calling from the landing. Instantly, Uncle Reuben let go of him and he found himself standing in front of the fireplace in the room above. His hair was standing on end and he was shaking. He ran to the door.

"Mum, thank goodness it's you!" he shouted. He'd never felt so glad to see his mother as he did when he opened the door to the landing.

"What are you doing? You know you're not allowed in this room. What if you had fallen through the floor? I can't trust you at all," she scolded as she pushed him along the landing. "Well, the ladies want to say goodnight to you and Polly, so get downstairs and then it's straight to bed!"

"But, Mum," he pleaded. Couldn't she see the state he was in?

All of the ladies, including the special guest, were getting their coats on and saying their goodbyes as Andrew stumbled down the stairs. Each one then proceeded to give both children a hug as they left and soon only the medium was left talking to Auntie Lizzie.

"Remember, dear," she said quietly to his aunt, "good fortune is coming your way. Your troubles will melt away and your life will be worthwhile again, mark my words."

Then she turned to Andrew.

"I have heard so much about you, Andrew. Give me your hand that I may touch it for luck."

Andrew reluctantly gave her his hand and she put something in it and closed his hand over it.

"Yours is a fine and noble quest," she whispered. "Be brave, but remember to keep this with you always. It will give you protection." And then she turned towards the door and, waving her goodbyes, left in the waiting car.

"What did the lady give you, Andrew?" Polly said as they were getting ready for bed.

"Nothing," he replied, but she had, in fact, given him a tiny pear-shaped crystal, which he promptly put in his handkerchief and placed in the bedside cabinet drawer. It didn't seem important, well, not as important as the ring that he was still wearing.

Once in the bathroom, Andrew could look at the ring in more detail. The diamonds sparkled brilliantly in the light and, again, it was marked with the Aldeton crest. Surely it was one of the jewels? Perhaps now was the time to tell his mother and Auntie Lizzie about what he had found in the secret room.

"Andy, won't you tell me what's been going on?" Polly said as he entered the bedroom. "I know I didn't believe you about the lane and the boy, but you looked as though you had seen a ghost when you came downstairs earlier."

Andrew stared at her. Could he trust her?

He took the ring off his finger and gave it to Polly. Then he told her everything.

"I can come with you next time you go to the secret room," Polly said, trying on the ring. "You said there was a small oriental pot to find. I could look for that while you search for the answer to the clue."

Andrew felt both defeated and relieved. He had hoped to complete the quest on his own, but he now realised that this would be impossible without Polly's help. Maybe he should have said something before.

Meanwhile, downstairs in the kitchen, Mum and Auntie Lizzie were clearing away the things from the buffet.

"Weren't you scared when Mrs G went into that trance, dear?" Mum said, putting the knives in the drawer.

"Not really," Auntie Lizzie replied. "I was just fascinated by the whole experience. I think her speaking to the ghost of Lord Alderton just made me feel sad. I've always known there was some sort of presence in the house, but I never thought he would try to get in contact. He must have loved his son Joshua very much."

"But didn't it make you afraid to carry on living here?" Mum asked again. "I know I was worried when she made those strange moaning sounds!"

"Oh, that was all part of the performance, dear," Auntie Lizzie said calmly. "I felt the only real thing was her knowledge of the house and its history. That was why the ghost managed to get in touch. It knew she would be understanding. Anyway, I'm glad Lord Alderton felt able to speak through her. He is my distant ancestor, after all. Mind you, I was disappointed that my husband didn't get in touch. I had a few questions I wanted to ask him. I still can't find some of his tools!" she laughed. "I think it's time for bed, don't you?"

# Chapter Eleven

It was still dark when Polly jumped out of bed and pulled the bedclothes off her brother.

"Wake up," she whispered, "time to go."

Both children put their dressing gowns on and Andrew, remembering the crystal that he had been given, put it in his pocket and used the torch to light their way along the landing.

The house was strangely quiet and even creepier in the half light. They could hear Mum snoring quietly as they carefully passed her door. She would be really cross if she woke up and found them!

"Remember, if you hear any strange noises, or see any strange shadows before I do, run back to the landing!" he whispered as he opened the door to the empty room. He was beginning to regret bringing his sister. He wondered if Uncle Reuben would attack her, too.

Polly nodded, but she was far too excited to think about such things.

As the stone steps were revealed, she followed Andrew down into the secret room and, as Andrew had done before, she stood and stared in wonder at all of the beautiful things before beginning her search of the drawers and cupboards.

In the meantime, Andrew went straight over to the bureau at the far end of the room. He was sure the answer to the clue was hidden there.

After searching every drawer carefully, though, there was nothing to be found and, trying to hide his disappointment, Andrew turned to help Polly with the china. There were different birds on each piece, but nothing as small as the pot that Joshua had described.

As there was no sign of the ghost, Andrew was getting anxious. Perhaps he was waiting for them to find the pot!

"I think we had better go back now," he said walking back to the steps. "Mum will be waking up soon."

Polly was disappointed at having to stop, but she reluctantly followed Andrew back up the steps.

Suddenly, her foot slipped and she fell backwards onto the floor below. She let out an ear-piercing scream, but the great roar that followed was even more frightening! Uncle Reuben was awake!!

Without thinking, Andrew leapt down the steps and pulled her up to the empty room. Then he half-carried, half-dragged her along the floor and through the door to the landing.

Once back in the bedroom, Andrew examined Polly's foot.

"You were so lucky. You could have broken it," he said. "I'm going back on my own next time!"

"You didn't help! Dragging me along the floor hurt more!" she complained rubbing her ankle.

"I shouldn't have agreed to let you come in the first place," he replied as he opened the bedroom curtains.

"But if you hadn't, I wouldn't have found this," Polly said triumphantly, showing him the small pot she had hidden in her pocket.

Andrew took it from her. Was it the right pot? Only Joshua would know.

# Chapter Twelve

"I've decided that we should go home at the end of the week," Mum said, gathering up the breakfast things. "You'll be starting a new term in September, so there's a lot to do. Besides, I have to get back to work."

Andrew and Polly looked at each other.

"Anyway," Mum went on, "I'm taking Auntie Lizzie shopping this morning and I'll be getting the rail tickets. I don't think you need to come, Polly, so you and Andrew can have some free time."

"Come on then," Andrew called later, as they watched the adults leave and soon both he and Polly were scrambling back through the hedge. Once the other side, they found Joshua who had been waiting patiently for news.

"And who is this delightful young lady?" he asked, bowing low to Polly who blushed profusely.

"This is my sister, Polly," Andrew replied, "she has something to show you."

Polly held out the Chinese pot for Joshua to examine.

"Yes," he exclaimed, "this is the pot I described! Give it to your aunt. Don't delay. It may be worth a small fortune!" and, with that, he disappeared into the mist.

"We must hurry now," Andrew said as they ran back to the house. "There's no time to waste."

Mum and Auntie Lizzie were in the lounge discussing the plans for their return to London when the children came rushing in.

"Auntie Lizzie, I think we can help you," Andrew blurted out.

"What did you say, dear?" she looked at him quizzically.

"Help me, what do you mean?"

"Andrew, if this is another of your tall stories we don't want to hear," Mum said. She had had enough of his vivid imagination.

"Auntie Lizzie," Andrew continued, "Polly and I found this and we think it could be worth a lot of money. You could use it to pay off some debts," he said as he carefully gave her the Chinese pot.

Mum was furious. How did he know Auntie Lizzie had money problems?

"I'm so sorry," she said apologetically to her aunt. "Andrew, that is really rude. Auntie Lizzie's affairs are nothing to do with any of us and where did you find that pot?" she shouted. "Was it in the West Wing?" then she turned to Polly. "I can't believe you've joined Andrew on this wild goose chase," she said in disbelief. "I'm so sorry, Auntie, I expect you'll be glad to see us go home after all their escapades!"

Auntie Lizzie wasn't listening. She was examining the pot with great interest.

She had recognised the design from some pictures she had seen in the library.

"Have you been in the West Wing, Andrew?" she asked him pointedly. "I thought I told you it was dangerous to go there."

"I'm sorry, Auntie," he said, "but I've been trying to solve a clue for Joshua and I think the answer is in the West Wing."

"It's that ghost story again. Don't listen to him," Mum said staring angrily at Andrew. "He had Polly and me looking for ghosts the other day. It was a total waste of time."

Polly stared at her mother. It was no good. For once, Polly had to defend her brother.

"But, Mum, that was ages ago. Things have changed. Andy is not making it up. It's true," she interrupted. "It's true that Joshua is a ghost, but I've met him and he needs our help to clear his name. Please listen to Andy. He can help Auntie Lizzie!"

"Well, Andrew," Auntie Lizzie said quietly. "Regardless of any ghosts, I would like to know what it's like in the West Wing, so let's go and have a look. Perhaps, you've found something really important."

Andrew was overjoyed. At last, someone was willing to believe him!

As they walked up the stairs, Auntie Lizzie held Andrew's arm. It was the first time she had attempted to climb them since her accident.

"You know there was a fire in the house hundreds of years ago. We must be very careful, Andrew. The floor in the West Wing is very weak," she said, gripping his arm even tighter. "I wonder how my lovely grandfather clock and the books survived the conflagration."

"I'm sorry, Mum," Polly whispered as they followed the others up to the West Wing, "I didn't mean to upset you, but Andy was so scared the other night that I felt I had to help him."

Mum said nothing. She was disappointed with both children. They had let her down. Ghosts indeed!

"Andrew, do you really want to go in that room again?" Mum said as they approached the door to the West Wing. She was hoping he would change his mind.

"Don't worry, Mary," Auntie Lizzie reassured her, "We'll be fine and if there's nothing to see, at least I will have satisfied my curiosity. Now, Andrew, let's see where you found this unusual pot."

Andrew was just about to open the door when he suddenly remembered the crystal.

"Won't be a mo," he said, running back to the bedroom.

Then, with his handkerchief and crystal tucked safely in his pocket, he ran back and followed everyone into the empty room.

"There's nothing here, Andrew," his mother said scornfully turning back towards the door.

"No, wait," he said, rushing over to the fireplace, "It's here," and no sooner as he had spoken than the floor opened and the steps appeared.

Auntie Lizzie and Mum stared in amazement.

"Are you sure it's safe to go down?" Auntie Lizzie asked anxiously.

"I think I'll wait up here," Polly said, remembering her fall. "Be careful, Auntie, the steps are a little slippery," and then she watched as Andrew, clutching his crystal, led the way down.

Auntie Lizzie, holding onto Mum's arm, stepped warily down into the secret room and then both women stared in silent wonder as the bright sunlight shone through the window at the end of the room revealing the beauty of the fine furniture and fittings.

"It's a miracle," she said, her face beaming with the joy of seeing the fabulous things. "I can't believe this has been here all this time and no one knew! Mrs G was right. She said good fortune was coming my way and she was right!" And as they continued to stare at everything, the morning light streamed through the window and the colours radiated in the sun's glow.

"I think you've solved all of my problems, Andrew," Auntie Lizzie whispered as she walked along examining the different things.

"I wanted to help you, but I want to help Joshua, too. I think his mother's jewels are hidden in the old bureau in that corner," he said, walking towards it.

"Who is Joshua?" Auntie Lizzie asked Mum quietly.

"He is my good-for-nothing nephew, madam," an eerie voice echoed behind them. No one had noticed the cold air and the darkness that had suddenly appeared all around them.

Auntie Lizzie and Mum froze as they heard the words. Then, they both watched in horror as the spectre of Uncle Reuben drifted towards Andrew who, taking his crystal out of his pocket, turned to meet it.

41

"I am not afraid of you anymore, Uncle Reuben," he said calmly then, instinctively, he held up his hand to show the crystal and the ring which was secure on his finger. The words that he spoke were not his own.

"Begone!" he shouted. "Begone from this place. This is not your time. It is our time, it is my time! Nothing here belongs to you. BEGONE!!"

As he spoke there was a terrible, wailing scream as the ghost of Uncle Reuben began to fade from view and then, without another sound, it disappeared through the outer wall.

For a second or two no one spoke, then Mum rushed over to Andrew and cuddled him.

"Why didn't you tell us what was happening?" she said holding him tight.

"I tried …" he said pulling himself free, "it's okay now. He's gone."

"I think I need to sit down," Auntie Lizzie said as she made her way back to the steps.

They hadn't noticed, but the room was again full of sunlight, even brighter than before. It was as though a curse had been removed and the room felt warm and inviting.

"What's going on?" Polly asked as they returned to the room once more. "You didn't tell me there was another ghost, Andy!"

"I didn't want to worry you," he said, as they walked towards the door to the landing.

Later, he told everyone about his quest to help Joshua and how he had met Uncle Reuben.

"I was hoping to solve the clue and find the jewels in the bureau, but there was nothing there," he told them. "I promised Joshua that I would help, but now I have no idea where to look."

"What's the clue, dear?" Auntie Lizzie asked. "I used to be good at riddles."

Andrew read out the clue and then, leaving everyone still

talking about the amazing things that had happened, he went back up to the bedroom.

He felt defeated. He had helped Auntie Lizzie, but he had failed Joshua.

# Chapter Thirteen

The weather during the next few days was appalling. It rained every day and the ground was so soggy that it was impossible to go out in the garden.

Meanwhile, a man had been to the house to see the incredible things in the secret room and Auntie Lizzie looked very happy because she had had everything valued and the furniture and the Chinese pot were so valuable that they would fetch more than enough money to pay off the mortgage and all of her debts. Auntie Lizzie was going to be a very rich woman.

Mum was still set on going home at the weekend and the idea of going home without helping Joshua was really upsetting Andrew. He and Polly had looked all over the house, but had run out of ideas since the ghost of Uncle Reuben had left the West Wing.

All too soon it was Saturday, the day they were going back to London. Both children had reluctantly got up early and, having packed, taken their cases downstairs. There were only a couple of hours left before the taxi would arrive to take them to the station. If only they had solved Joshua's clue.

Andrew stared out of the kitchen window in desperation. He needed to speak to Joshua once more.

"Can I go out in the garden before we go?" he asked. "I would like to speak to Joshua before we go. Coming, Polly?"

"Well, at least he is a kind ghost," Mum said, smiling. "I never thought I would be saying that! Don't forget, we're leaving soon!" she called after them as they sped out of the kitchen door.

Within seconds, they were scrambling back through the hedge.

"Why the hurry?" Joshua asked. He had been waiting for their return.

"We're leaving," Andrew said hurriedly, trying to explain what had happened to Uncle Reuben. "I'm sorry I haven't been able to find the jewels for you and now there's no time left."

"But time is the answer, Andrew," Joshua replied. "I solved the other clues and they spelt out the word 'clock' – 'look where time stands still' is the clock … my father's clock. You will find the jewels there and take these too," he said handing Andrew the pouch and his father's letter. "I will not speak to you after this as I feel my time in this place is nearly over. Thank you both for all you have done for me. It has been an honour to know you," and with that, he turned and walked back down the lane towards the cottage.

Auntie Lizzie was standing in the hall when the children came rushing in from the garden. She was staring at the grandfather clock and looking very sad.

"The time has gone so quickly," she said quietly, "but I'm so glad you both came to stay with me. I don't know what I would have done without you. I can stay in my home because of you. I'll miss all of you so much when you've gone."

But Andrew wasn't listening.

"Auntie," he said urgently, "can we look in the clock?"

"Why, dear?" she asked.

"It's important!" he replied, trying to open the casing.

"Yes, Auntie," Polly implored.

"Andrew, what are you doing?" his mother had come out into the hall from the kitchen.

"The answer to the clue is in the clock," he said wildly. "The missing jewels are in the clock!"

"Are you sure, Andrew?" Auntie Lizzie stared at him. "The old clock hasn't been touched in years. The door to release the pendulum is jammed. Nothing could be hidden in there."

"Ple-a-se can we open it?" both children shouted together.

"There's a key hanging inside the cupboard in the kitchen,

45

dear. Bring it to me," Auntie Lizzie sighed. Perhaps he was right. He did find the secret room, after all.

Andrew raced to the kitchen. Sure enough, there was a very ancient key hanging on a hook. He grabbed it and ran back to the hall.

"Let me try, Mum. I'm stronger than Auntie Lizzie." Mum nodded.

He put the key into the lock and started to turn it very carefully. It was a little stiff, but then there was a click and he was able to open the door to reveal a dark cupboard.

Andrew started to run his hand along the floor, but there was nothing there, but then, suddenly, at the back of the clock, he felt a lever. Instinctively, he pulled it towards him and the floor slid open to reveal a small compartment.

He pushed his hand deep into the gaping hole and pulled out a large velvet bag.

They stared in amazement as Andrew handed the bag to his aunt.

"It's for you, Auntie," he said proudly.

"I don't understand," his Aunt replied as she opened the bag.

"I know Joshua would want you to have them," Andrew continued, giving her the paper, "and this is a letter from his father which will explain everything."

Auntie Lizzie, having given the paper to Mum, proceeded to open the bag.

Everyone stared in wonder. It was full of jewels: diamond necklaces, emerald brooches, pearls and other precious and semi-precious jewels. Andrew had found the missing family jewels, but then the strangest thing happened. The pendulum in the clock began to swing. The clock started ticking. The grandfather clock was working again.

Out in the garden, the birds were chirping merrily. It was as though summer had returned. Green leaves filled the trees and the flower beds were full of beautiful flowers.

Everywhere was a feeling of joy and fulfilment and, as they stared out of the window towards the hedge, both Polly and Andrew saw the figure of a boy standing by the oak tree. This time he was dressed in the finest of clothes and beside him stood Sultan – on his back a fine, leather saddle. Suddenly, from out of the mist, a man dressed in a similar way appeared behind Joshua who turned to greet him. It was his father. They were together again at last.

The children watched and waved as both Joshua and his father bowed low to salute them before they and Sultan disappeared back into the mist for the final time.

The children stared at each other. They were sad to see Joshua go, but proud that they had helped him clear his name.

"I think I'm ready to go home now," Andrew told his mother as they got in the waiting taxi later.

# Chapter Fourteen

The weeks rolled by slowly after they had returned to London. The new school was okay, but both Andrew and Polly missed the freedom of Devon. It was no surprise that they had little enthusiasm for Christmas. There was nothing to do in the holidays and it was a time when they both missed their father.

"What have you got Mum for Christmas?" Polly asked as they walked home from school on the last day of term.

"I haven't got much," he replied. He thought he would give her the pouch that Joshua had given him. He had a feeling the odd stone might be worth something and he hadn't got a lot of money left since the summer holidays.

Mum was in the kitchen when they got back. She was holding a letter from Auntie Lizzie.

In it, she suggested lots of ways that Mum and the children could be a part of a new project she was planning, but Mum didn't want to rush into things. She would have to discuss it with her face to face.

"How would you like to share Christmas with Auntie Lizzie?" she asked as they walked in the back door.

Both children looked at each other, dropped their bags, and ran upstairs to pack.

"I didn't say we were going today," Mum said as she listened to the sound of drawers being opened and shut.

"We don't mind when we go," Polly said. "We just want to go!" and she and Andrew laughed. This was going to be the best Christmas ever and, maybe, this time they wouldn't have to come back!!

Lightning Source UK Ltd.
Milton Keynes UK
UKOW05f1343251116
288548UK00013B/328/P